dreamers

THE BOY
WHO PLAYED WITH
LIGHT

This book belongs to

_____

Read more in the Dreamers series by Lavanya Karthik

The Girl Who Loved to Sing: Teejan Bai

dreamers

THE BOY WHO PLAYED WITH LIGHT

SATYAJIT RAY

LAVANYA KARTHIK

duckbill

An imprint of Penguin Random House

For you, who sees stories in the world around them

PENGUIN BOOKS

USA | Canada | UK | Ireland | Australia
New Zealand | India | South Africa | China | Singapore

Duckbill Books is part of the Penguin Random House group of companies
whose addresses can be found at global.penguinrandomhouse.com

Published by Penguin Random House India Pvt. Ltd
4th Floor, Capital Tower 1, MG Road,
Gurugram 122 002, Haryana, India

Penguin
Random House
India

First published in Duckbill Books by
Penguin Random House India 2021

Text and illustrations copyright © Lavanya Karthik 2021

10 9 8 7 6

ISBN 9780143451525

Typeset in Georgia by DiTech Publishing Services Pvt. Ltd
Printed at Repro India Limited

www.penguin.co.in

It is the half shades, the hardly audible notes that I want to capture and explore.

—*Satyajit Ray*

Satyajit Ray made films that celebrated the play of light and shadow, daylight and darkness, joy and sorrow. His films changed the world of Indian cinema, and the way the world viewed it.

But this is not his story.

This is a story about the boy he was—a boy called Manik. A quiet, curious boy, with a big imagination and a great love for light.

Light was magic!

When it **danced** on the walls and floors of Baba's printing press.

When it *gleamed* on the great machines that made books and magazines come to life.

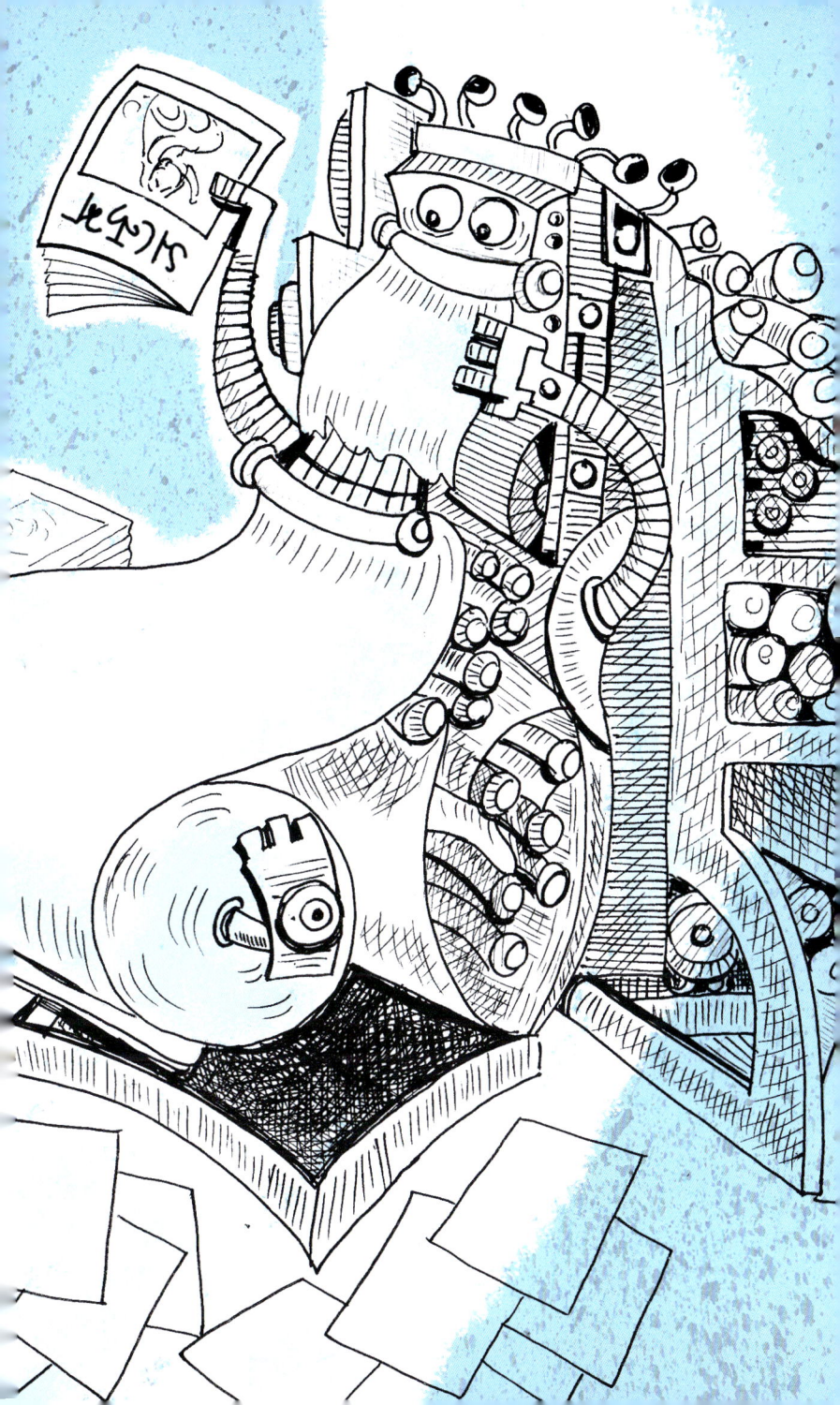

When it **shimmered** on the pages of the notebooks Baba filled with his poems and drawings.

I loved light. But then, the shadows appeared.

The shadows that settled under Ma's eyes after Baba died.

The shadows that pooled on the floor of the press as, one by one, the machines fell silent.

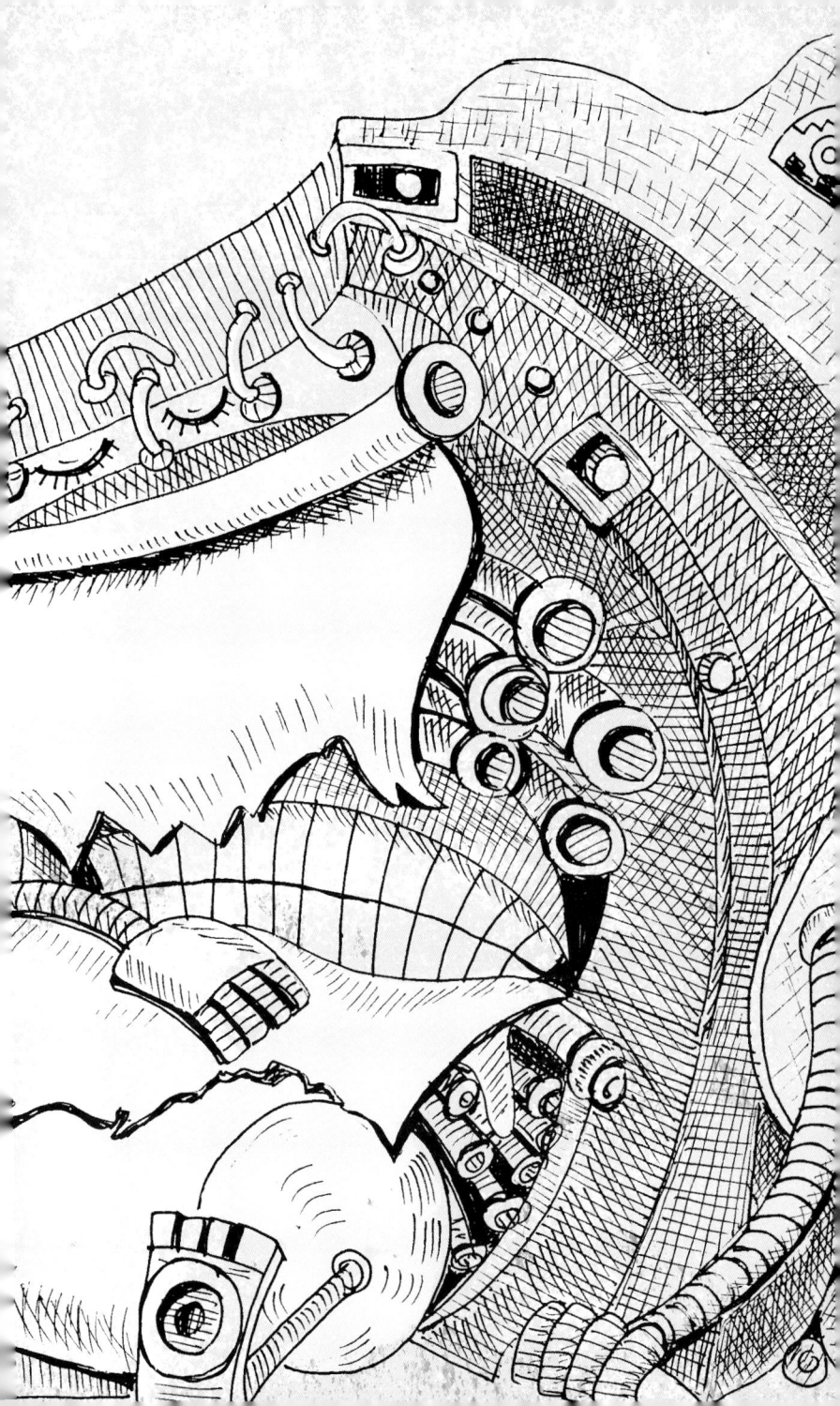

The shadows that watched from the corners, as Ma and I moved away.

There was light in the new home we made.

In the eyes of the family that welcomed us.

In the stories that Ma told me every night.

In the notebooks I filled with drawings, just like Baba once did.

But . . .

The shadows were always there.

They loomed in corners, watching me.

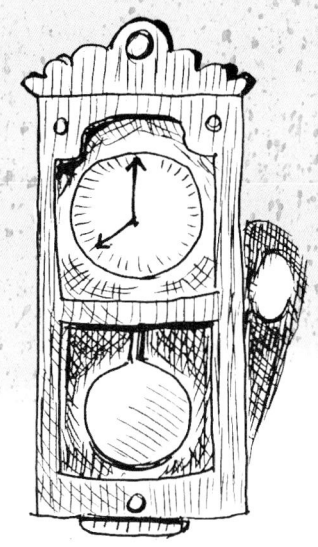

They *crouched*
under tables, muttering
and hissing.

I tried to describe them to my family.

My cousins chuckled. 'Manik will be a writer like his baba!'

The shadows **lurked** in doorways.

They **followed** me through the house.

I thought my drawings might help.

'What an imagination!' Ma smiled.
'Manik will be an artist like his baba!'

I raced through the house, up the stairs, down the corridors. The shadows followed!

'Manik!' my aunt called out, through the haze of the afternoon heat. 'Play quietly! We're trying to sleep!'

I dodged!

I dived!

An open door!

I threw myself in . . .

I slammed the door and . . .

Oh!

It was a reflection of the street outside—upside down and backwards!

The sky looked like the sea, the street was on the ceiling! People and buses soared overhead, birds swooped past my feet.

I lay there watching, till the light dimmed and the images on the wall faded into darkness.

'You're in here too, aren't you?' I said. The shadows stepped forward, nodding.

I looked at them. Then, I looked at them again—upside down and backwards.

They were stories, waiting for me to notice them.

'Talk to me,' I smiled.

And they did.

I returned to that room every day.
So did the stories. I watched and
listened, I wrote and drew.

I still loved the light, but now I sought out the shadows. In art and music, in dance and drama.

Most of all, in films.

When the time felt right, I turned to memories of those afternoons from my childhood.

'Let us tell the world our stories,' I said.

And we did.

This story is fiction, but based on fact.

Manik's father, the celebrated writer and artist, Sukumar Ray, ran the family printing press in Calcutta until his death, when Manik was barely three. The press and house were sold and Manik and his mother, Suprabha, moved to live with her brother, across town.

With no companions his age, Manik spent a lot of time alone while his mother was away at work. Luckily, he had his lively imagination for company.

What Manik saw in that room was fact too! Light through a tiny chink in the door entered the dark room and threw an inverted image of the street outside, on to the wall. This trick of light is called the pinhole camera effect.

Satyajit Ray's stories captured the tiniest of details, the subtlest of hues. His films, like rays of light, explored the shadows that make us human. And all of this might just have begun one hot afternoon, in a dark room lit up by a beam of light and his boundless imagination.

Satyajit Ray (2 May 1921–23 April 1992) is considered among the world's greatest creators of cinema. His first film was *Pather Panchali* (1955) and he directed twenty-nine feature films, five documentaries and two short films.

His films, especially those for children, such as *Goopy Gyne Bagha Byne*, remain well loved to this day. He also composed music, designed sets and costumes and made the posters for all his films. In addition, Ray was a much-loved illustrator and writer in Bengali, mostly for children and young adults.

He was awarded the Dadasaheb Phalke Award in 1984 and the Bharat Ratna in 1992. He also received an Oscar for lifetime achievement at the 64th Academy Awards in 1992.

The illustrations in this book are inspired by the art of Sukumar Ray and Satyajit Ray.

The author would like to thank
Pinaki De and Proiti Roy
for their invaluable help in the making of this book.

Lavanya Karthik is an author by day, a cookie monster by teatime and fast asleep by nine every night. She lives in Mumbai, where she writes, draws, eats a lot of chocolate and takes a lot of naps.